Magical Mayhem

Twink

Bimi

Pix

Sooze

Sili

Mariella

Kiki

Ivy

Book Twelve

Magical Mayhem

Titania Woods
Illustrated by Smiljana Coh

BLOOMSBURY

LONDON BERLIN NEW YORK

Bloomsbury Publishing, London, Berlin and New York

First published in Great Britain in 2009 by Bloomsbury Publishing Plc
36 Soho Square, London, W1D 3QY

A CIP catalogue record of this book is available from the British Library

ISBN 978 0 7475 9834 3

All papers used by Bloomsbury Publishing are natural, recyclable products made
from wood grown in well-managed forests. The manufacturing processes conform to
the environmental regulations of the country of origin.

Typeset by Dorchester Typesetting Group Ltd
Printed in Singapore by Tien Wah Press

1 3 5 7 9 10 8 6 4 2

www.glitterwingsacademy.co.uk

To Val, with love and thanks

Chapter One

It was the start of the new winter term, and Twink Flutterby was flying more slowly than usual as she travelled to Glitterwings Academy with her father and little sister, Teena. On the ground below trotted a salamander with a bright red harness around his chest. Twink held his lead proudly, watching him scamper along the winter-brown grass.

Teena had been flying some way ahead, but now she swooped back with her hands on her hips. 'Can't you *hurry*, Twink?' she complained. 'We won't get there until midnight at this rate!'

Twink shook her head. 'I don't want to tire Sal out – we've still got lots of work to do on our project once we get back to school.' She smiled down at the salamander, admiring his glossy black skin and vivid yellow spots.

Everyone in Twink's Weather Magic class had wanted to work with the school's salamander-thermometer for their winter term project, but Mrs Starbright had chosen *her*. Even better, Twink had been allowed to take the brightly coloured creature home with her over the holidays, so that she could start taking temperature readings with him. Twink and Sal had had great fun together over the last few weeks, and were now firm friends.

Teena rolled her violet eyes. 'Oh, bother Sal and your stupid Weather Magic class! That's all you've gone on about all hols – when you haven't been off measuring the temperature with him for hours on end.'

Twink looked at her little sister in surprise. 'Well, it's an important project! Everyone in our Weather Magic class is doing something to see whether

winter is coming later than usual this year, and then we're all going to present our results in a few weeks, and –'

'Blah, blah, blah,' interrupted Teena. 'I've heard it a million times already, Twink!' Before Twink could respond, Teena had darted away again.

Stung, Twink glanced at her father, who was flying nearby. From his expression, she knew he'd overheard. 'Um . . . I suppose I *have* talked about it a lot over the hols,' she admitted.

'Just a bit,' said her father with a smile. As usual, he was carrying both her and Teena's oak-leaf bags as he flew – and looked as if he'd be very glad to put them down!

'But Dad, it's really interesting,' said Twink eagerly. 'Did you know that we haven't even had a frost yet? Mrs Starbright says that's because the weather's getting warmer and warmer each year, and –'

She broke off. Her father's eyes were twinkling. 'Oh. I'm doing it again, aren't I?' she said sheepishly.

He chuckled. 'I'm glad you're enjoying your studies, Twinkster. Teena's just been feeling a bit left out, that's all.'

Father and daughter skimmed over the crest of a hill, with Sal trotting along below. Twink smiled as Glitterwings Academy came into view. The great oak tree stood on a hill of its own, its winter branches almost bare of leaves.

Even on a grey, cloudy day like this, Twink thought her school looked beautiful. Tiny golden windows spiralled up its trunk, and the grand double doors at its base stood open in welcome. Returning students hovered about the tree in colourful clusters, chattering and laughing.

As Twink and her father landed, Teena flitted back over to them. 'Dad, I've checked in already,' she said. 'I'm going to go up to Snowdrop Branch now with Zuzu, all right?' Zuzu was Teena's best friend, a fairy whose pink hair and lavender wings were the same as Twink and Teena's.

'I can tell you're heartbroken to leave your poor old dad!' said their father wryly, handing over Teena's bag and giving her a hug. 'Have a good term, then.'

Teena made a face. '*Anything* has to be better than how boring the hols were! Plus it took us so long to get here that I bet all the best beds are taken already.' She gave the salamander a dark look.

'You'd better hurry, then,' snapped Twink, patting Sal's head reassuringly. Usually she and her sister got on very well, but there were times when she wanted to throttle Teena!

'Don't worry, I'm going!' retorted Teena. 'Bye, Dad,' she added, kissing his cheek. 'See you later, Twink.' She skimmed off to where Zuzu was waiting near the entrance.

Twink let out a breath when she was gone. 'Let me guess – I need to be patient with her,' she said to her father. That's what Twink's mum was always telling her, though sometimes it was easier said than done!

Her father smiled. 'Well, no one ever said being the oldest was easy,' he pointed out, handing Twink her bag. 'But don't be too hard on Teena – she looks up to you a great deal, you know.'

'She has a funny way of showing it sometimes,' muttered Twink, adjusting Sal's lead.

Twink's father laughed and gave her a hug. 'Why else do you think she got her wings in a twist when you didn't have time for her over the hols?' he asked. 'Bye, Twinkster – have a good term. Send us a butterfly and let us know how you get on with your project!'

Twink stood waving as her father flew away. When she could no longer see him, she dropped her arm thoughtfully to her side. Teena was such an independent little thing that it was difficult to think of her looking up to Twink . . . but perhaps her father was right.

I'll make sure I spend more time with her this term, Twink resolved. Then she glanced at Sal, swishing his spotted tail about in the grass. *That is, after I finish the project,* she amended.

'Twink!' shouted a voice.

Twink grinned as her best friend Bimi Bluebell came fluttering up, her gold and silver wings glinting like sunshine. She landed beside Twink and the two fairies hugged tightly, bouncing up and down.

'It's so good to see you!' exclaimed Twink.

'You too,' said Bimi warmly. 'Oh, and look, here's Sal – hello, Sal!' she added, stroking the salamander's sleek head. Sal thumped his tail on the ground.

Twink grabbed her bag in one hand and Sal's lead in the other. 'Come on, I've got to get checked in with Miss Twilight,' she said. 'Then I need to take Sal back to his pen in the Creature Kindness log before we fly up to Violet Branch.' The fairies all lived and went to school high in the branches of the oak tree – much too far up for a salamander to be expected to climb!

'All right,' said Bimi, tucking a strand of midnight-blue hair behind her pointed ear. 'I've already been up to Violet Branch and saved our beds. We're making a three with Pix again – I thought we could swap notes on our project more easily that way.'

'Great!' said Twink happily.

Talking non-stop, she and Bimi flew over to the tree root where Miss Twilight stood checking in students. Twink's heart felt as light as thistledown.

It was wonderful to be back at Glitterwings. She could tell already that it was going to be a glimmery term!

'I can tell already that it's going to be a boring term,' said Teena glumly as she and Zuzu flew into the school.

The inside of Glitterwings Academy was like a high, golden tower, with fairies swooping in and out of its branches as far up as the eye could see. Teena almost groaned to see it again. Everything looked exactly the same as last term!

'Boring?' Zuzu looked at her in surprise. Her long pink hair was just the same shade as Teena's, though she wore hers pulled back with a leafy clasp. 'But why?'

Teena sighed as she and Zuzu began flying up the trunk towards Snowdrop Branch. 'Oh, I don't know,' she grumbled. 'Everything just *feels* boring. Twink spent the entire hols mooning about with that stupid salamander, and the weather's so dull and grey, and –'

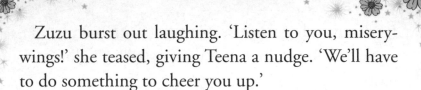

Zuzu burst out laughing. 'Listen to you, misery-wings!' she teased, giving Teena a nudge. 'We'll have to do something to cheer you up.'

Teena smiled despite herself. 'Sorry, I know I'm being a pain. But honestly, Zu, there wasn't *anything* fun to do over the hols. I almost died of boredom!'

She decided not to mention how hurt she'd felt that Twink had been too busy to do anything with her. Besides, she wasn't *that* bothered by it, Teena told herself. Let Twink do whatever she wanted – *she* didn't care.

'So anyway, now I want something really exciting to happen,' Teena went on firmly as the two friends landed on a ledge halfway up the tree. A single pearly-white snowdrop dangled over the door. 'That's my mission for this term. No boredom allowed!'

Zuzu giggled. 'Well, things are never boring with *you* around – that's for certain!'

The two girls pushed open the door to their branch. The curved bark walls were lined with mossy beds, with large white snowdrop blossoms hanging upside-down over each one.

Teena's spirits lifted to see two empty beds side by side with a fairy called Summer unpacking her things just beside them. What luck! Twink had once tried to throw the two of them together as best friends, which hadn't worked, but Teena still liked the orange-haired fairy very much.

The three fairies chattered away cheerfully as they unpacked. Summer grinned to hear of Teena's mission to do away with boredom. 'Well, that's good news,' she said, rubbing her purple wings together. 'We could use some fun to liven things up around here!'

'Look, what's that down on the ground?' said Zuzu, peering out of the window. 'It can't be a dandelion this late in the year, can it?'

'*Is* it? It's strange to have one so late in the season.' Summer joined Zuzu at the window. 'Ooh, it is! We should tell Miss Petal.' Their Flower Power teacher was mad about plants.

Holding back a groan at the pair of them, Teena placed a bottle of wing polish on her bedside mushroom. This was hardly what she'd had in mind when she said she wanted something exciting to happen!

'It's not that strange; it's just awfully warm still,' she explained wearily. 'We haven't even had a frost yet.' Then she winced. She sounded like Twink, rattling on about her project!

'You know, I've heard that humans use dandelions to do magic with,' said Zuzu, adjusting her hair clasp.

Teena paused in her unpacking. 'What do you mean? Humans can't do magic!'

Zuzu lifted a wing. 'Well, that's what I've heard. They blow on a dandelion, and if they can get all the seed pods to fly away in a single breath, they get a wish.'

'*Really?*' Teena joined Zuzu and Summer at the window, staring down at the dandelion. It was growing near the Fledge field, alone in a sea of grass. Its tiny white head bobbed in a gentle breeze.

Zuzu nodded. 'Yes, and the wishes really do come true for them – at least, that's what my gran says.'

Teena gazed at the dandelion in awe. A wish! How

thrilling! Fairy magic didn't include wishes, and the idea of a spell that gave you anything you liked was quite dizzying. In fact . . . Teena felt a tingle of excitement run across her wings.

'Humans are funny, aren't they?' Summer was saying. '*I've* heard that they make wishes on the first star to come out at night –'

'I've got a great idea!' interrupted Teena, beckoning her friends closer. 'If the dandelion magic works for humans, then why don't we try it? We could wish for anything we want!'

Zuzu and Summer exchanged a look. 'Um – I don't know, Teena,' said Zuzu slowly. 'It's *human* magic. What would happen if fairies did it?'

'Isn't it obvious?' cried Teena, fluttering her wings. '*We're* magic ourselves, so that should make the wish-magic even stronger! Come on, you two, what could go wrong? It's worth a try, isn't it?'

There was a pause. Finally Summer shrugged. 'Well, why not? It probably won't work, but we've got a bit of time before the opening session.'

'Exactly!' cried Teena triumphantly. 'What about

you, Zu? Are you coming with us?'

Zuzu bit her lip. 'We-ell . . . I suppose . . . it's just that in every story I've ever heard about, things always go wrong whenever someone makes a wish, and –'

'Those are just *stories*,' laughed Teena. Linking her arms through her friends', she flitted with them to the branch door. A moment later the three fairies were spiralling down the trunk, gliding past groups of returning students.

Seeing Zuzu's worried expression, Teena gave her a friendly squeeze as they swooped out of the front doors. 'Look, Zu, if it doesn't work, then no harm done – but if it *does*, we're going to have some fun!'

Up close, the dandelion was much larger than it had looked from the windows of Snowdrop Branch. Teena blinked to see that the white, fluffy head was half as tall as she was! It would be useless for the three of them to blow on it like a human, that was obvious.

'Maybe if we all sort of hover around it,' Teena

suggested. 'Then I'll make the wish, and we'll all flap our wings as hard as we can to make a breeze and blow the seed pods off!'

The three fairies arranged themselves around the dandelion's head. Summer looked amused, Zuzu nervous but excited. Teena took a deep breath. 'I wish that something exciting would happen!' she blurted out. 'Now, FLAP!'

The girls beat their wings in a frenzy, bobbing quickly about the dandelion. One by one, the seed pods began to take off, floating away into the air.

'It's working!' cried Teena. 'Keep flapping, keep flapping!'

More and more seeds took flight, until there was a steady stream of them drifting across the Fledge field. Finally there was only one seed pod left, clinging stubbornly to the dandelion's head. They had almost done it!

Teena hovered right next to it, flapping as hard as she could. At first she thought it wasn't going to work – and then all at once the last seed pod came away, spinning gently off after the others.

The dandelion's head looked naked and empty. Panting, the three girls collapsed on the ground and looked at each other, eyes shining. 'We did it!' crowed Teena, punching the air.

'Yes, but it's not *doing* anything, is it?' pointed out Summer with a grin. 'You asked for something exciting to happen, and –'

'Look!' cried Zuzu, grabbing Teena's arm.

Teena's eyes widened. A single large snowflake was falling through the sky. As she watched, it landed on the grass nearby, melting instantly. But then came another, and another. In hardly any time at all, the air was thick with snow.

'Oh, it's getting cold!' said Summer, jumping to her feet. 'Look, the snow's starting to stick to the ground already.'

The three fairies looked at each other in alarm. 'Um . . . you don't think this was because of my wish, do you?' said Teena uncertainly.

'I don't know,' said Zuzu, shivering. 'But we'd better get inside, quick!'

Her heart pounding hard, Teena flew with her

two friends back to the school, dodging the heavy snowflakes as best they could. The wind whistled around them, buffeting them every which way. She felt like a leaf swirling about in a stream!

Finally they reached the school, gasping in relief. Glancing over her shoulder as they sped through the double doors, Teena saw that the Fledge field was a blur of white.

The dandelion was gone, buried in the snow.

Chapter Two

The storm raged about the school, showing no sign of letting up. Students hung about the trunk's windows in excited clusters, staring out at the white whirlwind.

'I don't understand it!' said Twink. She and Bimi had been on their way to the Great Branch with the other Violet Branch fairies when the storm hit. They were now all hovering together at a window, all thoughts of the opening session forgotten. 'It was so warm when we first got here, and that was hardly *any* time ago!'

'Yes, our project's going to be interesting,' said Bimi thoughtfully. 'I'm supposed to be checking to see when the mice go into hibernation, but the poor things are probably as confused as we are now!'

'Well, I think there's something funny about it,' said Sooze. She had lavender hair and pink wings – the exact *opposite* of Twink, which was in fact their nickname for each other.

'What do you mean?' asked Pix, a clever red-headed fairy.

Sooze shrugged, her expression troubled. 'I've just never seen a storm come up so fast, that's all. It makes me wonder if there's something unnatural about it.'

A shiver of apprehension ran through Twink. The Violet Branch fairies looked at each other uneasily.

Suddenly the magpie's call echoed loudly through the school – three loud, insistent squawks. 'That means we need to get to the Great Branch!' said Twink. 'Come on everyone, we'd better hurry.'

The Great Branch was the largest branch in the school, with gleaming wooden floors and arched windows. Mossy tables were arranged in long rows, with a different flower hanging upside down over each one.

Twink's eyes widened as they swooped inside. Normally the Branch felt bright and airy, but now snow had piled up outside the windows, blocking out the light. If it wasn't for the glow-worm lanterns hanging overhead, it would be difficult to see at all!

As Twink headed for the Violet Branch table, she spotted Teena with some of her friends, looking pale and worried. Twink darted over to her. 'Teena, are you OK?' she whispered. 'It's just a storm – nothing to worry about!'

'Yes, I know,' mumbled Teena, not meeting Twink's gaze. 'I'm – I'm fine, Twink.'

Twink frowned. Oh, poor Teena! She was really scared. But before Twink could say anything else to comfort her, the HeadFairy's voice rang through the Branch.

'Everyone to your mushrooms, please,' called Miss Shimmery, hovering at the front of the room. The school's teachers sat on a platform below her.

'Promptly, girls – we need to get started!'

Hastily squeezing Teena's shoulder, Twink flitted to the Violet Branch table and sat on the spotted mushroom seat that Bimi had saved for her. An expectant silence fell over the Branch.

'Thank you,' said Miss Shimmery. Her rainbow wings shone in the dim light. 'Well – it may not have escaped your notice that it's snowing outside,' she said with a smile.

A relieved laugh rippled through the Branch. Twink felt herself relax. If Miss Shimmery wasn't worried, then everything must be all right!

The HeadFairy continued. 'Mrs Starbright estimates that the storm might continue for several days. School will begin as usual tomorrow, but outdoor classes are cancelled until further notice. The butterfly post service is also suspended until after the storm, as of course the butterflies can't fly in this weather.'

Twink listened carefully. Outside, the wind rattled at the windows as if it was trying to get in. The storm was beginning to feel exciting!

'Now then, on to our usual announcements.' Putting on her sparkle specs, Miss Shimmery peered down at a petal pad.

'School uniforms are required from tomorrow; Mrs Hover will be on hand to create them for the younger years. Students are reminded that oak-leaf caps must be worn at all times. No high-speed flying in the –'

THWACK!

Twink stifled a shriek as one of the windows banged open. A fierce gust of wind swept the room, blowing snow over some of the second-year tables. At the same moment the glow-worm lanterns went out. The room plunged into shadows.

Screams echoed throughout the Branch. Twink swallowed as she felt for Bimi's hand. The two friends clutched each other tightly.

'CALM DOWN!' commanded Miss Shimmery's voice, cutting through the panic. 'Is *this* how Glitterwings girls react to a bit of darkness? Calm yourselves, girls, this instant!'

A spark of light came from the platform. Miss

Sparkle, the Fairy Dust teacher, had conjured up a fairy globe – a light made of fairy dust. It grew larger as Twink watched, until it bobbed over the platform like a small sun.

The students were wide-eyed in the sudden light. Glancing at the Snowdrop table, Twink saw Teena's frightened face and longed to fly over to her. She must be terrified!

'Thank you, Miss Sparkle,' said Miss Shimmery. 'Mr Woodleaf, would you check the glow-worms?'

The Creature Kindness teacher flitted about the ceiling, peering into the lanterns. A moment later he touched down on the platform again and murmured something to Miss Shimmery. After consulting with the other teachers for a few moments, the HeadFairy addressed the school again.

'The glow-worms have been startled by the storm, and need to be left alone to recover,' she announced. 'They're sociable creatures, which means the school's other glow-worms will be affected as well. Since it's not practical to light the whole school with fairy dust, we've decided that the safest thing is for you all to sleep in the Great Branch tonight, where we can keep an eye on things.'

Sleep in the Great Branch? Surprised whispers filled the room.

Miss Shimmery smiled. 'It will be fun,' she assured everyone. 'I believe the humans call it a sleepover! After dinner Miss Sparkle will conjure up some bedding for us, and we'll get settled down.'

It was an odd dinner, with teachers and sixth-year students serving the food instead of butterflies. Twink felt a bit subdued as she and her friends ate their seed cakes and sipped fresh nectar. Outside, the storm still raged. The windows were now completely covered in white.

'It's a bit spooky, isn't it?' said Sili, a fairy with bright silver hair. She shivered dramatically. 'I hope no one wants to tell ghost stories tonight!'

A pointy-faced fairy called Mariella gave a superior smirk. 'You're not *scared*, are you, Sili? It's just a bit of snow!' Just then the window nearest their table gave a loud rattle, and Mariella yelped. They all laughed nervously.

Suddenly Twink thought of Sal, out in the Creature Kindness log with the school's other animals. 'I'll be right back,' she whispered to Bimi.

The Creature Kindness teacher was on his way out of the Branch when Twink caught up with him. 'Mr Woodleaf, will Sal and the other animals be OK?' she asked breathlessly.

Though clearly as nervous as he always was when speaking to his students, Mr Woodleaf managed a smile. 'Yes, ah . . . I'm just flying down there to check on them. Don't worry, Twink, they'll, ah . . . be fine.'

Twink sighed in relief as she flitted back to her table. It had been awful to think of Sal and the other creatures on their own out there, perhaps frightened by the storm.

Later, when the last crumb had been eaten and the oak-leaf platters all cleared away, Miss Sparkle magically created some cosy bedding for everyone as promised. The students settled on the floor, wrapped up in soft petal duvets. The fairy globe dimmed, filling the room with shadows.

Twink glanced over at the first-year area. Should

she check on Teena before she went to sleep? But her little sister seemed fine. She was talking with Zuzu and Summer, their three heads close together as they whispered.

Good, thought Twink with a smile. It looked like they were enjoying themselves.

She settled down between Bimi and Sooze. Bimi was already sound asleep, her midnight-blue hair spilling across her pillow.

'Goodnight,' murmured Twink to Sooze.

'Goodnight, Opposite,' Sooze mumbled back. Then she gave a soft laugh. 'It's been an interesting first day back, hasn't it? I wonder what the rest of the term will be like!'

Across the Branch, Teena was wondering the same thing. 'I can't believe that my wish caused all this!' she hissed anxiously to Zuzu and Summer. 'Do you think I'd get in lots of trouble if Miss Shimmery found out?'

'Don't worry, we'll never tell,' said Zuzu, rubbing her lavender wing against Teena's. 'It'll all be over in a few days anyway. No one will know it was you!'

Summer gave Teena a shaky grin. 'Well, I suppose you got your wish,' she said. 'This is pretty exciting, all right.'

'Hush, girls,' chided Mrs Lightwing, appearing beside them. 'It's time for bed now.'

Silence fell over the little group. Teena curled up in her petal duvet, her thoughts spinning. Yes, she had definitely got her wish! But Zuzu was right – it'll all be over in a few days anyway.

Wouldn't it?

Outside, the world was a shrieking whirlwind of snow. Birds sat huddled in bushes; hedgehogs took hasty shelter under piles of leaves; and in the trees the dryads shivered, feeling their sap slowing with the cold.

In the sky, a winged creature about the size of a cat was tumbling through the air, flapping and fluttering. A robin peeking out from a bush gasped in dismay. *A dragon!* The bird ducked quickly out of sight.

The young dragon didn't notice. The stinging snow was blinding him, and the wind whipped

cruelly at his wings. *Where was he?* Panicked, he called again and again for his parents . . . but the storm had blown him many miles away, so that he was now hopelessly separated from them by the raging snow.

What was he going to do? His parents had no idea where he was – and now the wind was blowing even harder, tearing at his wings and making it impossible to fly.

The young dragon landed clumsily on the ground, nearly turning a somersault in the snow. Almost immediately, the heat from his red scales melted the patch of snow around him, though the swirling flakes still stung his eyes.

The dragon peered around him miserably. He couldn't stay out here! It felt unnatural being so exposed – his usual home was a rocky cave that he shared with his parents.

To his relief, he spotted a small hole in the ground, not quite covered by a drift of snow. The dragon scuttled over to it, his spiked tail lashing back and forth. Fresh snowflakes began to cover the bare patch of ground behind him, coating it once again in white.

The dragon felt better the moment he was in the tunnel. It smelled faintly of rabbit, but he could tell that no rabbit had lived here for many years. Pointing his snout downwards, the dragon crept deeper and deeper underground, until finally he was in a small chamber lined with tree roots.

With an unhappy sigh, the dragon curled himself up tightly, tucking his nose under his tail. His heart ached as he thought of his parents. Even with their magic, how would they ever locate him down here? Yet he knew he'd had no choice but to take shelter. He'd just have to hope that they found him, somehow.

Closing his eyes, the dragon slowly drifted off into an uneasy sleep.

And began to dream.

Chapter
Three

The storm continued for two days – and then abruptly, on the morning of the third day, it ended. The students awoke to soaring blue skies, with sunshine sparkling on the snow like diamonds.

Like everyone else, Twink was relieved to hear that the glow-worms had finally recovered, and that the fairies could return to their branches. Sleeping in the Great Branch had been fun, but it was good to get things back to normal again!

'Brr, it's cold!' said Twink later that afternoon, rubbing her chilled wings together. She and Bimi were outside with Sal, measuring the temperature for their Weather Magic project. The salamander seemed unimpressed with the snow, sniffing at it disdainfully.

Bimi wrapped her thistledown scarf tightly about her neck. Like Twink, she was wearing a dress made of violet petals, with the bright yellow sash that showed they were third-year students. 'It's freezing!' she agreed. 'Do you have the temperature pad?'

Twink brought out the special petal pad that Mrs Starbright had given her. 'These results are going to be very different from the ones I took at home,' she said, flipping through the pad. 'I think the only thing our project's going to show is that the weather's gone completely topsy-turvy!'

She tugged on Sal's lead, and the salamander came scampering over. 'Here, Sal,' said Twink, showing him a fresh page. 'What's the temperature?'

Though salamanders couldn't live in fire as humans had once believed, they *did* love heat – and were experts on temperature! Sal stood very still for a moment, closing his eyes and twitching his tail.

Finally he touched his nose to the pad.

There was a swirl of golden light, and then the page turned a pale, icy blue.

'That's the coldest I've ever seen it!' exclaimed Twink. 'It looks like winter's properly here, all right.'

Bimi nodded. 'I checked on the mice this morning, and most of them have gone into hibernation already. I thought it would take *weeks* yet.'

'So did everyone else,' said Twink, tucking the pad back in her petal bag. 'It's strange how not even Mrs Starbright saw the snowstorm coming,' She frowned, remembering what Sooze had said. *Had* there been something unnatural about the storm?

Twink started to ask Bimi what she thought – and then saw that the salamander was standing stock-still, sniffing the air. Suddenly he took off at a run, jerking the lead from Twink's fingers.

'Sal! Come back here!' she shouted, flitting after him. Bimi followed close behind.

Sal's black tail disappeared around a low hill. Putting on a burst of speed, Twink jetted over the hill's crest – and then stopped in confusion.

'Bimi, look at this!' she cried.

The salamander was on a large, circular patch of ground with no snow on it. All around the circle, snowdrifts stood higher than the fairies – but where Sal had stopped, there was only grass.

Bewildered, Twink touched down beside him. What on earth did it mean?

'Oh, it's warm!' burst out Bimi as she landed. Twink blinked as she realised that her friend was right. The ground felt toasty under their feet!

The two fairies gaped at each other. Sal was trotting this way and that about the warm grass, sniffing excitedly at the ground. 'What *is* this?' said Twink. 'I thought that the school's dance circle was the only bit of enchanted ground nearby!'

Bimi shook her head. 'Maybe there's an underground hot spring here? We've never had such a heavy snow before, so that could be why we've never noticed it.'

'Maybe,' said Twink uncertainly. The patch was almost a perfect circle – would an underground hot spring do that? Even so, Bimi must be right, she

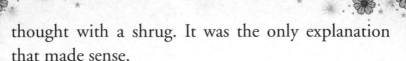

thought with a shrug. It was the only explanation that made sense.

Just then the magpie's call came from the tree. 'It's almost time for Flower Power!' exclaimed Twink. She grabbed the salamander's lead. 'Come on, Sal, I've got to get you back to your log.'

But Sal didn't seem to want to leave. He dug his feet into the ground, straining against the lead as Twink tugged. 'Come *on*,' huffed Twink. 'We're going to be late!'

Finally, with Bimi's help, they hauled the reluctant salamander away. Once back on the snow, he walked sulkily, dragging his tail behind him. As Twink shut him into his pen in the Creature Kindness log, he gave her a grumpy look and turned his back on her.

'I wonder what's got into him?' said Twink, once she and Bimi were speeding their way up the tree trunk to class. 'I've never seen him act that way before!'

Bimi shrugged as they landed on the Flower Power ledge. 'I suppose he just liked the warm ground over the hot spring,' she said. 'You know how salamanders love the heat.'

Twink's pink eyebrows drew together. 'Yes, but how did he even know it was there? It was really strange the way he –'

She broke off as the magpie's call shrieked again. They were late! Hastily, Twink pushed open the door.

Miss Petal, the young, pretty teacher who taught Flower Power, shook her head as they dashed in. 'Take a mushroom, girls.'

Once Twink and Bimi were settled, the teacher went on, 'As I was saying, I'm going to teach you a spell today that you can use on a single plant to learn the health of a whole forest. Ivy, would you help me pass these out?'

With the help of the green-haired fairy, Miss Petal gave an acorn pot to every student. In each one was a drooping plant. Twink's was a wilted fern, and she touched a curling frond with sympathy. Oh, the poor thing!

When everyone had a pot, Miss Petal continued.

'Now then, I'd like you to do a cheering-up spell as usual. Once your plants are feeling a bit healthier, I'll explain what comes next.'

Eagerly, Twink rested her hands on the fern's leaves. A cheering-up spell was one of the first she'd ever learned, but she never tired of doing them – it was lovely to see plants perk up!

Closing her eyes, Twink started to think happy thoughts. *Bright yellow sunshine. Birds singing. Laughing and sharing jokes with Bimi.* Her hands tingled as magic flowed from them into the fern. After a moment, she smiled and opened her eyes. There, that should do it!

'Oh!' she gasped. The fern was worse than ever! Ugly black spots had appeared all over its fronds, which hung limply over the pot's rim. As Twink gaped in shock, one of the fronds fell completely off, landing on her mushroom desk with a *plop*.

Sooze burst out laughing. 'Opposite, what did you *do* to it?'

'Nothing!' protested Twink. 'I just did the spell as usual!' She turned the pot around, but the fern looked just as awful from every angle.

'Oh dear,' said Bimi, biting her lip. 'It doesn't look very good, does it?'

Miss Petal came over. Her mouth twitched as she held back a smile. 'Twink, I don't think you could have had your mind on the spell,' she said gently. Putting her hands on the fern, she performed the magic herself. The black spots vanished as the fern burst into green, vibrant life.

'But – I'm *sure* I did it right,' said Twink in confusion. 'Honest, Miss Petal. I've done that spell a hundred times!'

Miss Petal nodded understandingly. 'Yes, but it's still easy to get it wrong, if your thoughts wander even just for a moment. Here, why don't you try again?' She produced another pot, this time with a drooping blade of grass.

As the class watched with interest, Twink placed her hands on the grass and redoubled her efforts, bombarding it with every happy thought she could think of. Sudden laughter made her eyes fly open. Oh, she didn't believe it! The grass had withered

until it was dried and brown!

'You must have something on your mind that's keeping you from concentrating,' said Miss Petal, quickly healing it. 'Never mind, Twink. You can take notes while I explain the technique; I'm sure you'll be able to try it out for yourself next time.'

'But –' Twink stared in frustration at the now-healthy blade of grass. Though she knew Miss Petal must be right, she could have sworn she'd performed the spell exactly the same as she'd always done!

Later at lunch, Sooze regaled the Violet Branch

fairies with the story. Even those who had been present in the class were soon howling with laughter.

'And then . . . she killed the SECOND one,' finished Sooze, waving her arms dramatically. 'Ker-plop! Dead! With the sheer power of her thoughts –'

'Sooze, it wasn't dead!' protested Bimi with a smile. 'Miss Petal was able to heal it.'

Sooze's eyes sparkled. 'Well, it's a good thing she was there, with Twink the plant-killer around!'

Twink laughed despite herself. She supposed it *was* pretty funny – though she still had no idea how she'd managed to mess up the spell so badly!

Just then Jade, Ivy's twin sister, stopped by their table. Ivy and Jade both had curly green hair, and looked exactly alike. If it wasn't for their different uniforms, Twink often thought that she couldn't have told them apart at all.

'What's so funny?' Jade asked, taking a seat beside her twin. She lived in Carnation Branch, and wore a frilly pink dress made of carnation petals.

'Oh, Jade, you missed it!' giggled Ivy, wiping tears

of mirth from her eyes. 'Go on, Sooze, tell the story again.'

Sooze grinned, leaning forward.

'No, *I'll* tell it,' groaned Twink, pushing her back. Briefly, she told Jade what had happened.

'Oh,' said Sili, blinking. 'That wasn't funny at all, the way you told it.'

'No, she hasn't got my magic touch with stories,' commented Sooze, taking a bite of seed cake.

Jade was frowning, ignoring the banter. 'But Twink, that's really weird,' she said slowly. 'The same thing happened to me in Fairy Dust class today!'

The table fell silent as Jade explained how she'd tried and tried to do a simple fairy dust spell, but it had gone wrong every time. 'Finally Miss Sparkle wouldn't even let me try any more, after I melted a hole in my mushroom desk,' she finished sheepishly.

Everyone burst out laughing. Pix grinned. 'You just need to pay more attention next time, Jade,' she said.

Glancing at her, Twink thought that Pix looked a

tiny bit smug. She and Jade were friends, but there was a good-natured rivalry between them to see who could get the best marks.

Jade tapped her wings crossly. 'I *was* paying attention. I knew exactly what I was doing, but I still couldn't make it work. It was like the spell had gone wrong or something.'

'But Jade, magic isn't like that,' said Pix, sounding maddeningly reasonable. 'Either you do it right or you don't, that's all.'

'I *was* doing it right!' insisted Jade. 'And I thought it was just me, but if the same thing happened to Twink –'

Pix snorted. 'Oh, come on, Jade! Isn't it possible that you and Twink just made mistakes?' She spun on her mushroom seat. 'Twink, there wasn't anything strange about it, was there? You just made a mistake, that's all!'

Twink hesitated. Like Jade, she had been certain that she'd done the spell correctly – but as Miss Petal had said, it only took a moment for your thoughts to wander. Maybe she really *hadn't* been

51

concentrating properly.

'I'm not sure,' she admitted, playing with her oak-leaf plate. 'I *thought* I did it right, but . . . but I suppose I must not have.'

'There! You see!' said Pix triumphantly.

Jade rolled her eyes. 'Fine, Pix, have it your way,' she said. 'But *I* think there's something strange going on around here!'

Chapter Four

A few days later, Twink was in the Creature Kindness log with Sal, grooming him with a piece of soft moss until his black and yellow skin gleamed. Normally the salamander loved this sort of attention, but today he stamped his feet restlessly.

'Sal, what's wrong?' asked Twink finally, putting down the moss. The Creature Kindness log was where all the school's animals lived, and Sal had always seemed happy there before.

The salamander scampered to the window of his pen and gazed out. Twink stared at him. Sal's every muscle was tight and alert, as though he was watching something.

Joining the salamander at the window, Twink frowned as she peered out across the snowy landscape. She couldn't see a thing!

'What is it, Sal?' she said.

He gave her an incredulous look, as if he couldn't believe that Twink didn't see what he saw! Propping his front feet on the window sill, Sal stared even more intently, his shiny black nose touching the glass.

Utterly bewildered, Twink looked out of the window again, scanning the snowy meadow and the wood beyond. *What* was Sal looking at? Whatever it was, he seemed completely fascinated!

White flakes spiralled downwards as a light snow began to fall. Suddenly Twink's eyebrows drew together. *Had* she seen something? There, on that little hill! There was the faintest of shifting movements – like something white and ghostly, drifting against the snow.

The snowflakes began to fall more heavily, hiding whatever it was from view. A moment later, it was as if Twink had never seen the ghostly movement at all. *Maybe I didn't*, she thought in confusion. It had been so subtle –

Twink jumped as the magpie's call came from the tree. 'Sal, I've got to go to class,' she said, quickly gathering up her things. 'I'll be back later, OK? We'll go outside and take some more temperature readings.'

Sal didn't move from the window. As Twink flitted from the log, she looked over her shoulder. The black and yellow creature was still exactly where she had left him, staring outwards.

'And begin!' directed Madame Brightfoot, sweeping her arms into the air.

Standing in a circle with their wings touching, the Snowdrop Branch fairies began to dance. Madame Brightfoot's class took place outdoors, in a ring of mushrooms near the wood. Protected by magic, the little circle was always bright and sunny, with soft grass underfoot.

Teena smiled to herself as she dipped and spun. It was nice to feel that things were back to how they should be. Perhaps she hadn't wanted excitement as much as she'd thought!

'Lovely, lovely! Now, up we go!' called Madame Brightfoot. A curl of purple hair tumbled down from her bun.

The fairies fluttered upwards, continuing to perform the graceful steps. Teena waited expectantly for the golden sparkles that gathered whenever a magical dance was being performed.

But nothing happened. The air remained clear, with only a few stray dust motes drifting past.

Madame Brightfoot frowned. 'Someone is not paying attention! Again, girls, from the start. We will do it correctly this time!'

Teena and Zuzu glanced worriedly at each other as the fairies glided back down to the ground. 'Do you think –' Zuzu started, and then fell silent as the dance began again.

Teena performed the steps woodenly. Several of their friends had had problems with spells over the last few days, but that had just been a coincidence! It *couldn't* have had anything to do with her wish . . . could it?

Teena swallowed hard as the fairies took to the air again. *Oh, please, let there be sparkles this time*, she thought fervently. *Just one or two would do – something to show that the magic's working!*

But there were none. The other Snowdrop girls looked at each other in bewilderment.

'Oh, you naughty fairies!' burst out Madame from the ground. 'Who is not paying attention? Land! I shall show you how to do the dance myself!'

The fairies landed. Teena nibbled the side of her

thumb as they watched Madame perform the dance. She lifted up into the air with a flourish, her red wings glinting.

'And now we shall have the sparkles!' she announced, posing dramatically in place.

Teena gazed hopefully upwards. Not a single sparkle appeared.

Madame blinked. 'And now . . . the sparkles!' she repeated, striking her pose again.

As if in answer, a lump of snow fell from a branch overhead, landing wetly on the grass in the centre of the circle. A gasp ran through the Snowdrop fairies as a stray snowflake drifted down beside it – and then another.

'Ooh, it's cold!' squealed a fairy called Reni, clutching at her arms. Teena gulped. She had never particularly liked Reni, but she couldn't deny that the green-haired fairy was correct – the temperature in the magic circle was dropping by the second.

'But we're supposed to be protected here,' whispered Summer.

Madame Brightfoot looked pale. 'Class

dismissed!' she cried, clapping her hands. 'Hurry, children, back to the school. I must speak to Miss Shimmery immediately!'

She sped off towards Glitterwings, with most of Snowdrop Branch racing after her. Teena lagged behind, staring dumbly at the lump of snow on the ground. Her wings felt too leaden to move.

Zuzu tried to smile. 'Wow, Teena! When you make something exciting happen, you don't mess around, do you?'

'Oh, don't *say* that!' pleaded Teena, spinning towards her. 'You don't think this is happening because of my wish, do you? It can't be! My wish only brought on the storm, that's all!'

'Well . . .' Zuzu trailed off as she and Summer exchanged a glance.

Teena's blood chilled. 'You *do* think it's because of my wish,' she whispered.

Reluctantly, Summer lifted a wing. 'Tee, what else could it be? Everything's been weird since you made it.'

'Then I'll make another wish, and change things

back to the way they were!' burst out Teena. 'Come on, you two – help me find a dandelion!' But snow covered the ground in a soft, thick blanket. Try as they might, the fairies couldn't find any flowers at all.

Zuzu put her arm around Teena. 'Don't worry, I'm sure the teachers can put things right!'

'But I can't *tell* them,' protested Teena, wringing her hands. 'I'd get into so much trouble – I can't even imagine how much!'

'I bet you won't even need to tell them,' said Summer reassuringly. 'They've got *loads* of magic, especially Miss Shimmery. Now that they know something's up, they'll sort it just by waving their wings!' She did a pirouette on the snow, fluttering her purple wings.

'Really?' said Teena. 'Do you really think so?'

'Of course!' said Summer. The three friends started back towards the school. 'Just wait and see. When it comes to magic, there's nothing the teachers can't do.'

'Definitely,' agreed Zuzu as they swooped through the double doors. She linked her arm through

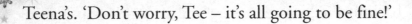

Teena's. 'Don't worry, Tee – it's all going to be fine!'

The Great Branch was unusually subdued during lunch that day. All over the school, it seemed, spells were going wrong. At each table, the fairies whispered worriedly, swapping stories of magical mayhem.

'See, Pix, Jade was right,' said Ivy at the Violet Branch table. 'There *is* something strange going on – it's happening to everybody now!'

Pix's cheeks reddened as she nodded. 'Yes, it looks like she was. But – but I just don't understand it! Magic *always* works, if you do it correctly . . .' She trailed off, biting her lip.

'Not any more,' said Sili softly. 'We couldn't get *any* of our spells to work in Fairy Dust class today. Miss Sparkle finally dismissed us, and went to see Miss Shimmery.'

Twink's stomach tightened. The same thing was happening all over the school – but the possibility of magic not working was unthinkable, like the sun refusing to rise! What could it mean?

'It all began with that storm,' pointed out Sooze. She picked up her seed cake and then put it down again, pushing her oak-leaf plate away. 'I still say there was something strange about it, coming up out of nowhere like that.'

'Well, I think the teachers should *do* something,' burst out Mariella, her pointed face pinched with fear. 'Why do our parents send us here, if something like this is allowed to happen? I've a good mind to write to my mother and –'

'Oh, hush, Mosquito Nose,' snapped Sooze. 'You don't suppose the teachers are letting it happen on purpose, do you?'

'Twink,' whispered Bimi from behind her wing, 'do you think that strange patch of grass we found might have anything to do with it? We thought it was because of a hot spring, but . . . well, what if it's not?'

Twink frowned, remembering the warm circle of earth that Sal had seemed so excited by. 'I don't know,' she muttered back. 'Maybe we should –'

'Your attention, please!' called Miss Shimmery.

All talking ceased as the school turned towards the HeadFairy. Every face in the room looked tense, and eager for answers.

Unlike the night of the storm, Miss Shimmery's face was now grave. 'I'm sure you're all aware that there have been problems with magic occurring in the school,' she said. 'The teachers and I will be working our hardest to correct this, but meanwhile, all classes are dismissed until further notice.'

An uneasy murmur swept through the school. Twink gulped.

'Students are *not* to attempt to use magic – *any magic at all* – until the problem is sorted,' continued Miss Shimmery. 'Hopefully we'll locate the source of the problem quickly and things will return to normal, but if not, you will all need to be sent home.'

There was a stunned silence. '*Sent home?*' whispered Sili, looking close to tears. 'But –'

'Meanwhile, I want you all to try not to worry – but *do* use your Glitterwings good sense,' finished Miss Shimmery. 'Stay close to the school, and don't go anywhere on your own. Now then, if the teachers would please come with me –'

Miss Shimmery flew towards the door in a flurry of rainbow wings, followed by the Glitterwings teachers. Only Mrs Hover the Matron remained, comforting some of the younger students.

'Twink, I think we should tell her about that patch of grass!' hissed Bimi urgently. 'It might mean something!'

'You're right – come on!' said Twink, leaping from her seat. The two friends flitted after Miss Shimmery, but before they could reach her, Mrs Hover called them back.

'Not now, girls,' she urged, flapping heavily over to them. 'Miss Shimmery is very busy right now.'

'Yes, but we've got something important to tell her!' cried Twink. Across the Branch, the HeadFairy vanished through the doors, with the teachers flying after her.

Mrs Hover glanced at the younger years' tables, and then ushered Twink and Bimi closer to her.

'Listen, my lovelies,' she whispered. 'Miss

Shimmery and the other teachers have gone to try and fix the tree's magical protection. If they can't do that, then anything you have to tell them won't matter a whit! Now, do try and finish your lunches – we all need to keep our strength up.' She bustled off, patting her pink hair worriedly.

Twink and Bimi gaped at each other. 'The tree's magical protection?' whispered Bimi as they started back towards their table. 'But if *that's* not working . . .'

Twink's wings felt clammy. The tree's magic kept Glitterwings and its nearby grounds shielded from

all sorts of dangers. Without it, *anything* could happen!

'What was that about, Opposite?' demanded Sooze as they sat down again. The rest of the table were gazing at them, too, their expressions a mix of curiosity and fear.

Twink and Bimi exchanged a glance – and decided in the same moment not to worry the others unless they had to.

Twink managed a shrug. 'Nothing,' she said, picking at her seed cake. 'We just wanted to ask if we could do anything to help, that's all.'

Teena felt cold as she watched Miss Shimmery and the other teachers fly from the Great Branch. She had thought that the adult fairies could solve the problem easily – but clearly, this wasn't the case.

'Did you see how worried they all looked?' whispered Zuzu, her violet eyes wide.

'It looks really serious,' agreed Summer. She swallowed. 'Teena, I know it would be awful for you, but – but maybe . . .' She trailed off.

Dread swept over Teena as she realised what her friends were thinking. She *couldn't* tell what she had done; she just couldn't! 'Come on, let's finish our lunches,' she said hurriedly. 'Then we'll go to the library. Maybe we'll find an answer in there!'

Chapter
Five

The Glitterwings library was a tall room with shelves that stretched to the ceiling. Quite a few students had gathered here on this strange afternoon with no classes, though not many seemed to be looking for books. Instead they sat at the mushroom tables in worried clusters, whispering together.

Teena and her friends waited until Mrs Stamen's attention was elsewhere, and then flitted into the Restricted section.

'What are we looking for?' asked Zuzu doubtfully, gazing up at the lofty shelves.

'Anything that might help!' Teena pulled out a book at random, flipping through its petal pages. No, that one was no good! She shoved it back into place.

Summer was looking more methodically, reading titles out loud. '*Befuddled, The Magic of Confusion* . . . *Advanced Biped Transformation* . . . *Spells on the Wing: Mid-Flight Magic* . . . Hang on, what's this?'

She took down a dusty volume with an old, cracked spine. '*Wish Spells*,' she read, her voice rising in excitement. 'Oh, Tee, I think this is it!'

Teena and Zuzu darted to Summer's side as she opened the book to its table of contents. '*Chapter Seven: When Wishes Go Wrong*,' read Teena in wonder. 'Summer, you star!'

Taking the book from Summer, Teena shoved it under her uniform. She peeked out to check that Mrs Stamen wasn't watching. 'Come on!' she hissed.

With her friends following, Teena flew to an empty table in the corner. Trying to look casual, she spread her wings. 'There, now no one can see what we're doing!' she whispered, taking the book out.

The three girls huddled together as they read the strange, old-fashioned words. Teena blinked as she saw that the chapter was mostly about *humans* who had made foolish wishes. Apparently fairies in olden times used to grant wishes to humans, though she couldn't imagine why. The humans seemed to have messed it up every single time.

Like me, I suppose, thought Teena, her cheeks reddening. Her wish hadn't been very clever either!

'Wasps! Who would have thought that there are so many ways for wishes to go wrong?' murmured Summer, turning a page. 'Teena, look – here's something!'

The girls leaned forward. '*Inexact wishes and how to reverse them*,' read Teena. Holding back a shout of delight, she bounced on her mushroom seat. 'Oh, Summer, that's it, that's it! Now I just have to do the spell, and everything will be all right again.'

'But –' started Zuzu, frowning.

Teena was already scanning the instructions. 'And it's an easy one as well. All I have to do is say it out loud, and imagine what outcome I want. Perfect!'

'Well, do it in a hurry – Mrs Stamen will notice us in a minute,' urged Summer.

Zuzu tapped her wings together. 'Wait a minute, you two! There's something we've forgotten about –'

'Zu, we haven't time!' said Teena. Quickly committing the little rhyme to memory, she closed her eyes and imagined that her wish had never happened.

She began to speak. '*If wishes were horses, then beggars would ride, but a foolish wish one must deride. If a horse is a beggar and the beggar's a horse, then the wish must be reversed, of* – MMPH!'

Teena spluttered to a stop as something clamped over her mouth. Her eyes flew open, and she pushed her friend's hand away. 'Zuzu, what are you doing?' she cried. 'I almost had it!'

'Yes, and what would have happened then?' demanded Zuzu. 'Tee, Miss Shimmery told us not to do *any* magic. And that's because all the spells are going wrong! So why do you think *this* one would go right?'

Horror prickled at Teena's wings as she saw what

Zuzu meant. 'Oh!' she gasped. 'If *this* spell went wrong too, then –'

'Yes, exactly!' said Zuzu. 'Things might get even worse than before!'

Summer hurriedly shut the book. 'Oh, Zu! I'm so glad you thought of that – Teena and I were being a pair of wasp brains!'

'Then that means we can't do anything at all,' said Teena slowly. *Except tell the teachers the truth*, she thought. But that was still too awful to contemplate, and she went on in a rush, 'So – so I suppose we'll just have to wait, and hope that the teachers can –'

She stopped as an unfamiliar noise came from outside.

'What's *that*?' said Zuzu, her eyes wide.

The three friends flitted to a nearby window. Teena's mouth fell open as she saw that two humans were coming up the hill. *Humans!* But no humans had ever been here before – the tree and its surrounding area were protected by magic!

Teena's heart hammered in her chest as she watched the humans approach. There was a man and a woman, both wearing boots and carrying walking sticks. They seemed to be arguing.

'You see?' came the man's voice. 'I *told* you you're not reading the map properly. You didn't even know this hill was here, did you?'

'It's not! Here, look for yourself.' The woman thrust a folded-up piece of paper at him. The two of them consulted it.

'Well, that's strange,' said the man. 'We should be in Parson's Field now! How on earth did this hill and that wood get here?' He squinted up at Glitterwings, and Teena shrank back against the window.

'See, I told you!' laughed the woman, taking the folded-up paper back. 'Less about my map-reading skills next time, hmm? It must be a printer's error or something.'

Teena's head swam dizzily. Humans, *here* – and it was all her fault! Beside her, Zuzu and Summer looked just as stunned and frightened as she felt. The humans began walking up the hill towards the school, talking and laughing.

'What's that noise?' said a second-year student. Suddenly a small crowd had joined them at the window – and a moment later, there was chaos.

'Mrs Stamen! Mrs Stamen! There are *humans* out there!' shrieked a purple-haired fairy.

'*What?*' The librarian hurried out from behind her mushroom desk. 'Oh!' she gasped.

Teena felt herself jostled from all directions as everyone clustered around the windows to see. Dozens of wings stirred the air as fairies took to the air to get a better view.

'Oh, it's true!' cried another girl. 'They're coming

this way! Mrs Stamen, what should we do?'

'Teena!' hissed Zuzu, shaking Teena's arm. 'You *have* to tell now – you just have to!'

Teena nodded weakly. But before she could get the words out, Mrs Stamen had flown into action. 'Get away from those windows!' she shouted, clapping her hands. 'The library's closed – I have to go and find Miss Shimmery immediately.'

'Mrs Stamen, I – I mean, there's something –' stammered Teena.

'Hurry, Teena!' urged the librarian. 'Go back to your own branches, all of you!' she called out. 'Go, go!'

The fairies streamed out of the doors in a flurry of different-coloured wings. 'Mrs Stamen!' cried Teena, close to tears. '*Please* – I have to –'

'Not now!' The librarian swept Teena and her friends out of the library and into the trunk, banging the doors shut behind her. 'There's no time – the humans might –'

'AAAGGGHH!' screamed a voice.

Whirling about, Teena saw a fourth-year student

pointing at a window in the trunk. 'There's an eye up there! Something's looking in!' The girl burst into tears, and Mrs Stamen flew quickly to her, shepherding her away.

'You girls! Go to Snowdrop Branch this instant!' she called over her shoulder as she sped off.

Teena hovered in place, staring in frightened fascination at the blue-green eye peering into their school. As she watched, the eye vanished – only to reappear at another window further up.

'Isn't it amazing!' said the man's voice.

'I don't believe it!' said the woman's from the opposite side of the tree. 'Why, the windows go all the way up!'

'Oh!' yelped Zuzu, whirling about. 'They're on both sides! There's another eye up there, a brown one!'

'We *can't* fly past them to Snowdrop Branch,' gasped Summer. 'Quick, you two – in here.' She pulled Teena and Zuzu behind a large knothole. They hovered together, trying to make themselves as small as possible.

Peering around her, Teena saw that they weren't the only ones hiding. Frightened fairies had taken refuge in every knothole and bend of the trunk. As a terrified stillness fell over the tree, the humans' voices could be heard more clearly.

'But what *is* it?' said the man. Teena winced as a banging sound reverberated around them like thunder. The man was knocking on the school with his fist! 'Listen, it's hollow,' he said. 'But the tree's *alive*! How can that be?'

'Maybe – maybe it's some sort of art installation,' suggested the woman doubtfully. 'You know, like something in a gallery.'

'But the hill wasn't on the map!' said the man, sounding frustrated. 'And see here, Martha – there are *doors* at the bottom. Look how tiny the hinges are!'

Peeking downwards, Teena saw one of the front doors open. She held back a shriek. The man's finger was in their school!

'There's a floor – and it's *polished*,' he said. 'I can feel how smooth it is! I don't know what we've found, but . . .' He trailed off. To Teena's great relief, his finger disappeared, though the door stayed open.

'I . . . I don't know either,' said the woman. 'Frank, if I didn't know any better, I'd think that something actually *lives* here!'

There was silence. Risking another peek, Teena saw that the windows were all clear now. Were the humans gone at last? But then the man's voice came again.

'Typical – I've left my mobile in the car! We'll have to go back. We need to get the press out here, pronto.'

'You mean, ring the papers?' said the woman, sounding surprised.

Press? Papers? Teena strained to hear.

'Of course!' said the man. 'This should be studied. If there really are – well, fairies, or pixies, or something – then the public deserves to know!'

'I suppose you're right,' said the woman. 'How exciting!' Their voices began to fade. 'I wonder how much we'll get for selling our story to them?' she said . . . and then they were gone.

Almost immediately, the magpie's call rang through the school – three long, urgent caws. Up above, Miss Shimmery appeared, diving down the trunk with the other teachers behind her.

'To the Great Branch!' shouted Miss Shimmery as she flew past. 'Everyone to the Great Branch, hurry!'

Chapter
Six

Twink and her friends had been in the third-year Common Branch when they first heard the humans' voices – and had stared down in horrified fascination as the couple prowled about the tree.

'*Humans* – oh, what could be worse!' moaned Sili.

Twink bit her lip. By mistake, she had stayed in a human house for over a week the previous winter, and had learned that humans really weren't that bad. Some of them, like the little girl Twink had befriended, were lovely – though it was true that the adults could be a bit dense sometimes!

A shudder ran through Twink as she remembered how Lindsay's parents had thought she was a moth at first, and tried to swat her. What would happen if *these* humans realised that they'd found a whole school full of 'moths'?

Sooze had opened a window and was half-hanging out of it, listening to the conversation down below. 'They're leaving!' she cried. 'But they're talking about coming back with something called *the press*. What's that, Opposite? Do you know?'

Twink shook her head as everyone crowded anxiously around her. 'No, I've never heard of –'

The magpie's call rang through the school, interrupting her. 'That's the signal for us to go to the Great Branch!' cried Pix. 'Come on, everyone, hurry!'

'I am afraid that the situation is now grave,' announced Miss Shimmery once the entire school was assembled. Almost two hundred frightened fairies stared back at her, not moving so much as a wing tip between them.

'Sadly, the other teachers and I were unable to mend the tree's protective spell, and now humans have found us,' said Miss Shimmery. Twink gulped as she saw the HeadFairy's expression. She had never seen her look so sorrowful, or so serious.

'This leaves us with only one choice,' continued Miss Shimmery. 'We must evacuate the school immediately.'

Alarmed murmurs broke out. Miss Shimmery went on, raising her voice. 'Stay with your year

groups, and go immediately with your year heads to the wood. From there, we will send word to your parents to come and collect you.'

Bimi raised her hand. 'But Miss Shimmery, what will happen to Glitterwings?' she cried.

'Yes, the humans were talking about something called the press,' burst out Sooze. 'What *is* the press? What are they going to do?'

This was what the whole school had been wondering. Unconsciously, every fairy in the Branch leaned forward, their faces tense.

Miss Shimmery took a deep breath. 'The press is the humans' communication system,' she told them. 'The two humans who found our school are planning to tell the rest of their kind about us.'

A horrified gasp ran through the Branch. *Every human*, knowing about Glitterwings? Perhaps even coming to see it for themselves, poking and prying about? Twink's heart turned to ice as she imagined it.

'As to what will happen to our beloved school . . .' Miss Shimmery's voice wavered, and then she straightened her rainbow wings firmly. 'We cannot say yet – and we have no time to discuss it. Quickly, girls, we must leave! Go with your year heads. And do NOT return to your branches for any belongings first – time is of the essence!'

Bimi's face looked pinched and anxious as everyone scrambled up from their mushroom seats. 'Twink! I've got to go and get Chirpy,' she whispered. 'He's not a belonging, he's a *creature* – I can't just leave him!'

Twink nodded. 'Come on,' she said, grabbing Bimi's hand. 'We'll go and tell Miss Twilight; she'll understand.'

The third-year head was a tall, imposing fairy with silver hair and purply-grey wings. Despite the urgency of the situation, she listened carefully as Twink explained about Chirpy.

'Yes, go on – but be quick!' she said. She was standing on one of the mushroom seats, counting the third-year class. 'Go together, the pair of you, and then come to the wood immediately.'

As Twink and Bimi flew out of the Great Branch,

a voice called, 'Twink! Twink, wait!'

Twink whirled about as her little sister came speeding up. 'Teena, what are you doing?' she demanded. 'You heard Miss Shimmery – go to the wood with the rest of your year!'

Teena looked close to tears. 'I know, but – oh, Twink, you don't understand! I tried to tell Mrs Lightwing, but –'

'Teena Flutterby!' Mrs Lightwing herself appeared, bobbing beside them with a face like

thunder. 'You must come along this instant – we're leaving!' Behind her, the first-year students were already exiting the Great Branch, flying out in a double-line formation.

'Yes, but –' Teena got no further. Mrs Lightwing took her by the shoulders and firmly propelled her out of the Branch.

'You girls hurry, too!' she ordered over her shoulder. 'Flitter-flutter, get a move on!' She and Teena went through the doorway, disappearing from view.

Twink and Bimi looked at each other. 'What do you suppose Teena wanted to tell me?' asked Twink worriedly.

Bimi shook her dark blue head. 'I don't know. Come on, let's go and get Chirpy! We'll see Teena in the wood; she can tell us there.'

The two friends sped out of the Great Branch and up the trunk. The upper part of the tree felt empty and abandoned. Below them, long lines of fairies raced downwards, leaving the school as fast as they could.

Barely even pausing to land on the Violet Branch ledge, Twink pushed open the door and they rushed into the room, half-flying and half-running to their beds. Bimi's cricket-clock sat on her bedside table as usual, looking anxious.

'Chirpy! Oh, you poor darling – were you terrified?' cooed Bimi, sweeping him up in her arms. He chirped in relief to see her, snuggling into her embrace.

Twink grabbed Chirpy's cage. 'Come on, hurry!' she said.

Bimi carefully put Chirpy into his cage and fastened the latch. Though she knew she shouldn't, Twink took her favourite drawing of her family from her bedside mushroom.

'Let's go,' she said, tucking it into her petal bag. 'The others are probably long gone already!'

The two fairies sped down the length of the trunk. It felt even quieter than before, and Twink realised that apart from herself and Bimi, the tree was deserted.

'Oh, Twink, I'm scared!' breathed Bimi, clutching

Chirpy's cage to her chest.

Twink swallowed. 'I know – me, too,' she said. 'But we'll be with the others in a few minutes, and – *oh*!' She broke off as a sudden horrible thought came to her. 'Bimi!' she gasped. 'What about Sal? He'll be so frightened – I've got to go and get him, too!'

Bimi's eyes widened. 'But Miss Twilight told us to go straight to the wood –'

'Yes, but I *can't* leave Sal,' insisted Twink. 'And what about the other animals in the Creature Kindness log? I have to check that they're all right!'

They flew through the double doors and out into the cold winter day. Bimi nodded. 'OK, but I'm coming with you – Miss Twilight said to stick together!'

The two friends jetted down the slope to the Creature Kindness log, the icy wind whistling past their wings. Twink landed with a hop, and pushed open the door.

'Mr Woodleaf!' she exclaimed. The green-haired teacher looked up distractedly as he fastened a lead on to a mouse's harness. Several sixth-year girls were bustling about the log as well, obviously getting the animals ready to leave.

Twink felt herself relax. She should have known that the Creature Kindness teacher would never abandon his beloved animals!

'Twink! Bimi! What are you two doing here?' Mr Woodleaf flitted over to them. As always, he sounded much more confident when he was with his animals. 'You need to get to the wood with the rest of the school!'

Twink nodded. 'I know, sir – I was just worried about Sal.' The salamander was watching Twink longingly from his pen. Noticing this, Mr Woodleaf opened the pen door and Sal scampered out, frisking delightedly around her.

'Here,' said Mr Woodleaf, attaching Sal's lead and handing it to her. 'He'll be happier with you, and I know you'll keep him safe. Now *hurry*, both of you – the humans might come back at any time!'

The wood was only a short distance away, but their flight was agonisingly slow. Once out of the log, Sal seemed excited by something over the next hill, and kept tugging sideways on his lead.

'Sal, *stop* it!' gasped Twink, yanking him back again. 'What's wrong with you?'

The salamander whined, his short legs pedalling the ground.

'Bimi, you go on ahead!' said Twink desperately. 'There's no need for *both* of us to be out here.'

'Don't be silly. Of course I'm not going to leave you!' Tucking Chirpy's cage under one arm, Bimi grabbed Sal's lead as well, pulling on it hard. '*Move*, Sal – we're in danger, don't you understand?'

Suddenly Twink saw something: a thin, wavering mist rising up against the blue sky. It was the same mist she had seen once before, from the Creature Kindness log. 'Bimi, look! What *is* that?' she said.

Bimi gave it a hurried glance. 'I don't know – is it smoke? Hurry, Twink; you're as bad as Sal!'

Twink gazed down at the lizard-like creature. He was staring back at her, imploring her to understand. 'Sal . . . is there something important about that smoke?' she asked. He jerked against his lead in

answer, trying to drag her closer to it.

'Who *cares*?' burst out Bimi. 'Twink, we have to go! The humans are probably on their way right this second!'

Twink shook herself as she realised her best friend was right. She was certain that something strange was going on – but now wasn't the time to work it out.

She tugged at the salamander's lead. 'Come on, Sal. We'll check it out later, I promise!' A sudden lump formed in her throat. Would there even *be* a later, once the humans' 'press' got involved?

She pushed the thought away. 'Let's both pull at the same time,' she said to Bimi. 'Ready? One . . . Two . . .'

'TWINK!' shouted Teena's voice. Twink's mouth dropped open as her little sister came zooming up.

'Teena, what are you *doing* here?' cried Twink. 'Get back to the wood with the others!'

'No, I – I have to tell you something!' cried Teena, her violet eyes bright with tears. 'Oh, Twink – this is all my fault!'

Chapter Seven

'*Your* fault?' repeated Twink in confusion. 'What are you talking about?'

Teena began to cry, choking the words out. 'Oh, Twink, I – I wished on a dandelion on our first day back – and I wished that something exciting would happen – and the moment I did, the snowstorm started, and now all this, and – and oh, what have I done?' She wailed the last words, covering her face with her hands as she sobbed.

Dropping Sal's lead, Twink quickly put her arms around her little sister. 'Hush, don't cry,' she soothed. 'But Teena, I don't understand. What do you mean, you wished on a dandelion?'

Sniffling, Teena explained about the human magic that Zuzu had told her about. 'I know I shouldn't have tried it,' she said. 'But I was fed up, and – and I wanted something different to happen.'

Twink frowned. She knew from her time with the humans that, unlikely as it might seem, they *did* have magic – Christmas and Santa Claus had taught her that. Mixing fairy magic with a human spell seemed a sure recipe for trouble – but even so . . .

'Teena, I don't see how your wish could have caused all this,' said Twink slowly. 'Your magic just isn't strong enough yet, even if the fairy magic and the human magic *did* go wrong together.'

'It sounds like her wish probably caused the storm though,' put in Bimi. She was struggling to hold Sal's lead on her own as he strained and pulled.

Twink nodded, thinking hard. 'Bimi, I wonder if – if maybe the *storm* caused something to happen somehow.' The smoke wisped against the sky, teasing her. *What* did it mean?

'But how could a snowstorm – *oh*!' cried Bimi as Sal jerked his lead from her fingers. He raced off over the hill.

'Sal, come back!' shouted Twink. 'I've got to go and get him,' she said frantically. 'Teena, go straight back to Mrs Lightwing, and tell her exactly what you've told us! And explain that I had to go after Sal –'

Twink shouted the last words over her shoulder as she shot off. A moment later she realised that Bimi was flying just behind her. 'I'm not letting you go alone!' panted Bimi. 'I gave Chirpy to Teena – she's going to go and get the teachers.'

Despite her fear, a sunny warmth spread through Twink. Bimi was the best friend in the world!

They zoomed over the top of the hill . . . just in time to see Sal's spotted tail disappear down a hole in the snowy ground. The smoke they had seen was coming from the hole's entrance, rising out in a thin, steady plume.

Twink and Bimi landed in a skidding stop. 'It's a rabbit hole,' said Bimi, peering in. 'Sal! Sal, come

out this instant!' There was no reply. They could just hear the sound of the salamander pattering away down the hole, his footsteps growing fainter and fainter.

'What do you suppose is causing the smoke?' said Twink, gazing at it uneasily.

Bimi rubbed her silver and gold wings together. 'I don't know, but . . . Twink, isn't that patch of melted snow close to here? It's just over the next hill, isn't it?'

The same thought occurred to both girls at the same time. 'It's not a hot spring at all – there's something

down there!' burst out Twink.

'And Sal's gone in after it!' Bimi's blue eyes were wide with horror.

Twink took a deep breath. 'Bimi, I've got to go and get him. Mr Woodleaf trusted me to keep him safe! You don't have to come – I know how scared you are of going underground –'

Bimi looked pale. 'No, I'll come,' she said softly. 'I'd never forgive myself if I didn't, and something happened to you.'

Twink started to argue . . . and then looked into the dark rabbit hole and thought better of it. The last thing she wanted to do was to venture down there alone!

The two fairies edged into the hole, holding hands tightly. The dirt tunnel sloped sharply downwards, so that they had to flutter their wings to keep their balance. The daylight winked out behind them as they rounded a bend.

'Sal!' called Twink into the darkness. 'Sal, come back!'

There was no answer. Bimi squeezed Twink's

hand. 'Let's keep going,' she whispered.

They tiptoed onwards. Suddenly Twink realised that it was growing warmer with every step they took, like walking into summer. Before she could mention it, a hot breeze gusted through the tunnel, stirring her hair.

'Bimi, did you *feel* that?' she gasped.

'It's like something's on fire!' agreed Bimi's frightened voice.

The scorching breeze came again, and again. *Oh please, let Sal be all right*, thought Twink as she and Bimi edged their way downwards. It felt as if they were walking into a human furnace! What on earth was down there?

The two fairies felt their way along the warm dirt wall as they rounded another curve. Twink jumped back with a shriek.

Staring at her out of the darkness was a pair of bright orange eyes.

For a terrifying moment, Twink thought they belonged to some sort of monster . . . and then her eyes adjusted to the chamber's dim light.

'It's a *dragon*,' she breathed. Those orange things weren't eyes at all. They were his nostrils, glowing with fire! Smoke curled from them in long grey tendrils.

The dragon was asleep, with Sal snuggled up beside him. Salamanders and dragons were cousins, remembered Twink suddenly. No wonder Sal had been so excited by the dragon's presence!

Another sizzling breeze blew past as the dragon let out a soft snore. 'I didn't know that there still *were* any dragons!' exclaimed Bimi.

Twink nodded. 'Just a few, my father says. He's

very young, isn't he? The poor thing must have got lost from his parents in the storm!'

They crept forward until they were almost close enough to touch him. The dragon's scales were a rich golden-red that glowed in the faint light. Suddenly he whimpered in his sleep, his feet and tail twitching.

'Oh, he's having a bad dream!' said Bimi. She started to stroke the dragon's claw, and then jerked her hand away. 'It's *hot*!' she exclaimed.

'My father says that dragons are the most magical creatures of all,' said Twink, gazing at the slumbering beast in awe. 'He says their magic is *much* stronger than fairy magic. In fact –'

Twink broke off suddenly, her eyes widening. 'Bimi! Do you think maybe his magic has been interfering with ours somehow? I mean – if he *did* arrive in the storm, then it all started once he got here, didn't it? It could all be because of him!'

'Oh, Twink, you could be right,' gasped Bimi. 'Especially if he's upset and having nightmares! We've got to get him away from here – as quickly as we can.'

The two fairies stared up at the snoring dragon. Twink bit her lip. 'Er . . . how shall we wake him up?' she said. She was fairly sure that it was a bad idea to startle a dragon awake – he might blast them with his fiery breath!

Bimi gulped. 'Um . . . dragon?' she called softly. 'Hello, dragon . . . Wakey, wakey!'

The dragon didn't stir. Picking up a twig from the ground, Twink very cautiously prodded the dragon's leg. 'Dragon, do wake up!' she implored. 'It's important!'

She flitted backwards as another red-hot snore gusted past them. *Ouch!* 'Bimi, what are we going to do?' she hissed, flapping her wings to cool them. 'We've *got* to wake him up.'

Uncurling himself, Sal cocked his head to one side as if listening to them. His eyes twinkled – and then all at once he leapt up on to the dragon!

'Sal!' cried Twink. 'Get down from there!'

The salamander scampered nimbly up the sleeping dragon's back. Despite the heat, Twink's wings felt like ice. What was Sal *doing*?

Suddenly jets of orange flame burst from the dragon's nostrils as he started awake. Twink and Bimi shrieked, darting backwards.

The dragon lifted his long neck and peered closely at Sal, perched on his back. Salamander and dragon regarded each other for a long moment – and then Sal crept even nearer.

Twink's jaw dropped open. Why . . . he was whispering something in the dragon's ear!

'What's he saying?' murmured Bimi, craning to see. As if in answer, the dragon turned and stared at them with a pair of large golden eyes.

Twink managed a weak smile. 'Er . . . hello!' she said, waving.

The dragon's spiked tail thudded on the dirt floor. Uncoiling himself, he lumbered to his feet. His bat-like wings fluttered hopefully.

Sal slid down the dragon's snout and scampered across to the fairies. 'Oh, Sal, well done!' praised Twink, stroking his smooth head. 'You clever thing – you've made him understand!'

'Will he follow us, do you think?' said Bimi,

scratching the dragon's nose with a stick. He closed his eyes, almost purring with pleasure.

'One way to find out,' said Twink, picking up the salamander's lead. 'Come on, everyone – we have to hurry!'

The dragon followed readily, trundling after the fairies as they headed upwards through the tunnel. At least he seemed to be making an effort not to breathe fire on them, thought Twink – though she did let out a squawk once when he sneezed, blasting a super-hot breath at their heels!

Finally they emerged on to the snowy hill. The afternoon was drawing to a close, and the sun hung low in the sky. 'Twink, look!' cried Bimi.

Twink's wings sagged with relief as she saw Miss Shimmery, Mrs Lightwing and Miss Twilight flying towards them in the distance, along with Teena, who was showing the way.

'We're here!' she called, shooting up into the air and waving her arms. 'We're – AAAGGGHHH!'

Twink screamed as a gust of wind roared over her

like a hurricane, sending her flailing head over pixie boots. Fluttering her wings madly, she righted herself – and her jaw dropped.

Landing on the ground beside the rabbit hole were two adult dragons, each the size of a human house. Steam hissed from the ground as the snow melted around them.

Twink gaped, taking in the dragons' gleaming red scales and glittering eyes. It was the breeze from their massive wing strokes that had bowled her over, she realised – she hadn't stood a chance against it!

Shooting happy jets of flame, the young dragon threw himself at his parents, nuzzling and purring. The adults enveloped him tightly with their wings. A lump formed in Twink's throat. How worried the little dragon's parents must have been!

She touched down lightly beside Bimi and Sal. 'Isn't it glimmery?' she whispered from behind her hand. 'They're back together again!'

Bimi nodded vehemently. 'Good old Sal,' she said, patting his head. 'You knew what you were doing, didn't you?' Sal swished his black and yellow tail, smiling to himself. At the top of the hill, the teachers and Teena had stopped, watching the scene in amazement.

Finally the largest dragon's head came up. Peering towards the sunset, he narrowed his eyes. A moment later, all three dragons were taking off into the air. The little dragon dipped close to Twink and Bimi, his face alight with joy.

'Goodbye, dragon!' called Twink, waving as hard as she could. 'I'm really glad that you've found your parents.'

The adults nodded to the two fairies, saying *thank you* with their eyes. A moment later, all three dragons were flapping away silently over the wood, the little one zooming playfully about his parents.

In no time at all, Miss Shimmery and the others arrived, landing in a flurry of brightly coloured wings.

'*What* has been going on?' demanded the HeadFairy. 'First Teena's been telling us about her unfortunate dandelion wish, and now there are *dragons* here?'

Hastily, Twink and Bimi explained what had happened, their words rushing over each other. The HeadFairy tapped her rainbow wings together thoughtfully. 'A young dragon, not yet in control of his magic, having nightmares . . . Yes, that would certainly be enough to disrupt our own magic!'

Miss Twilight's cloak glittered with moonstones as she nodded. 'I suppose his parents couldn't find him sooner because the magic around the tree was in such chaos – it would have thrown off any spell they were doing. But then, once it broke down completely, they were able to locate him.'

'Oh, poor little dragon!' burst out Teena. 'It was all my fault, wasn't it? If I hadn't caused the storm with my wish, he wouldn't have got lost!'

Twink's heart went out to her sister – but before she could say anything, a low rumbling noise reached their ears, growing louder every second.

Mrs Lightwing took to the air. 'It's a car!' she called down grimly. 'The humans are back. They're driving one of their awful vehicles right across the hills, heading straight for us!'

Chapter Eight

Miss Shimmery swung into action. 'Now that the dragons are gone, we may be able to save our school!' she said. 'We've no time to put the magical protection back into place before the humans get here – but Gloriana, could we perhaps cast a glamour spell?'

Miss Twilight nodded as the car roared closer. 'Yes, if we're quick! I'll need all of your help – Twink, you and Bimi, too!'

Twink gulped. Though she and Bimi had studied Star Magic for almost a year now, they were hardly experts at the tricky art of illusion.

'But Miss Twilight, don't we need starlight to cast a glamour?' said Bimi fearfully.

'Usually, but we'll have to make do with what we have!' Miss Twilight ushered them all together, apart from Teena. 'Now then, everyone, the humans will have seen our hill already, so our only hope is to convince them that Glitterwings is an ordinary oak tree – *completely ordinary!*'

Teena watched anxiously from the sidelines as the others began to cast the glamour spell. Their eyes were all closed as they made strange, intricate motions with their hands and wings. *Oh, please let it work, please!* thought Teena, biting her lip.

Meanwhile the car's engine had been drawing closer and closer, roaring angrily through the air. Suddenly it stopped, leaving an ominous silence.

Teena started as three car doors slammed shut on the other side of the hill, one after the other. The humans were almost here! Beside her, Sal crouched low to the ground, looking as frightened as she felt.

The huddle of fairies were now holding hands, not moving a muscle as they cast their spell. Was it taking effect? Hugging herself, Teena craned to hear the approaching footsteps.

'There it is. Wait till you see it up close; you won't believe your eyes!' said the man's voice.

The spell wasn't working. Holding back a sob, Teena stared up at Glitterwings, rising up against the blazing sunset. Oh, if only there was something she could do to help! Any moment now their school would be seen, and it would be too late.

Suddenly Teena's attention was drawn by a tiny flickering in the evening sky. The first star had come out, shining faintly. All at once, Summer's words came back to her – *sometimes humans make a wish on the first star.*

Teena gulped. Another wish spell. Did she dare, after last time?

'Hold on, let me get my camera ready,' said a male voice, so close now that prickles ran over Teena's wings. 'Mate, you and your missus better be

right – this place is in the middle of bloomin'
nowhere.'

'Oh, we are; just wait and see!' said the woman.
'Come on, we're almost there.'

The footsteps trudged closer. Teena glanced at the
other fairies, and saw that Twink and Bimi were
beginning to tremble with the strain. Their spell
wasn't going to work!

I've got to do it, Teena thought frantically. *It might
be our only hope.* But she couldn't make a mess of it
again – she had to wish carefully this time!

Taking a deep breath, Teena gazed up at the first
star and closed her eyes. *I wish that Miss Twilight's
glamour spell would work, so that the humans don't see
our school and they go away from here!*

Slowly, Teena opened her eyes again.

At first nothing seemed to have happened . . . and
then another tiny star appeared in the sky, winking
alongside the first. And then another. Suddenly
there was a small handful of twinkling stars, shining
starlight down on to the circle of fairies.

As Teena watched in wonder, silvery flakes of

magic began to gather around them. The sparkling flakes swirled upwards, growing larger and larger, until the entire hill was enveloped in a glittering silver sphere.

'Here we are!' said the man's voice. 'I bet you've never seen anything like *this* before.'

Teena's heart dropped down to the ground. *It still hadn't worked.*

'No, I certainly haven't,' replied the other man. 'An oak tree! Well, blimey, that's front page news. Stop the press; there's an oak tree growing in the countryside!'

'What do you . . .' The first man's voice trailed off. 'Martha, the windows are gone!' he burst out.

'But it was different before!' gasped the woman. 'Honestly, Mr Taylor! It – it had little windows, and doors, and –'

'And a polished floor! Something lived in there!' babbled the man.

'Uh-huh,' said Mr Taylor drily. 'What a waste of time – you're both nutters!' His footsteps stomped off back down the hill.

There was a long silence.

'Martha, I – I don't feel very well,' said the man finally. 'Let's go home, and have a nice cup of tea.'

'Yes, and I want extra sugar in mine,' mumbled the woman. 'I think I'm having a funny turn, Frank.'

Teena drooped with relief as the couple staggered off. At her side, Sal swished his tail joyfully. A moment later they heard the car doors bang shut again, and then the vehicle roared off.

The circle of fairies jumped into life. 'Hurrah, we did it!' shouted Twink. She and Bimi hugged tightly, bouncing up and down. 'They've gone, they've really gone!'

'Oh, well done, everyone!' breathed Mrs Lightwing. 'I'll go and tell the other teachers, so that we can get the students back into school where they belong!' She sped off towards the darkening wood, with Miss Twilight following after her.

'Yes, well done, girls,' said Miss Shimmery warmly to Twink and Bimi. 'However, if I'm not very much mistaken, we had a bit of help with that spell.

Teena, do you want to tell us something?'

Teena felt her cheeks catch fire as Twink and Bimi looked at her in surprise. 'I – I made another wish,' she confessed, rubbing her wings together. 'Summer told me about another piece of human magic – wishing on stars. So – so I sort of did.'

Miss Shimmery looked grim. 'Teena, human magic is *extremely* unpredictable! Nobody knows much about it – least of all humans themselves. It is *not* something for fairies to be meddling in, do you understand? Anything might have happened!'

'Yes, Miss Shimmery,' mumbled Teena, staring down at her pixie boots. She looked quickly up again as she heard a soft chuckle. Why – Miss Shimmery was *laughing*!

'Having said that, I'm rather glad that you *did* decide to meddle with it again, just this once,' admitted the HeadFairy with a wry smile. 'That extra starlight gave us just the boost we needed for the spell to work. What was your wish?'

Teena told her, and Miss Shimmery nodded in approval. 'A much more exact and carefully thought-out wish than your first one. I take it that you see now how foolish it was to wish for "something exciting" to happen, without specifying *what*?' She straightened her sparkle specs, gazing sternly at Teena.

Teena squirmed. 'Yes,' she said in a small voice. 'Yes, I really do, Miss Shimmery. I – I know that this whole thing was my fault.'

'Not entirely,' corrected the HeadFairy. 'The snowstorm was the direct result of your wish – but like all things, it had consequences, and the poor young dragon got caught up in them. That's why it's so very foolish to cast a spell without knowing *exactly* what you want the outcome to be.'

'I understand,' whispered Teena. She couldn't bear to look at her sister, or Bimi. How disappointed they must be in her! She took a deep breath. 'Will – will I be expelled?'

'Expelled?' Miss Shimmery sounded surprised. 'Your only crime was to be very foolish, Teena. If I started expelling my first-year students for *that*, I'd soon not have any! But you should have told us the

moment you realised what had happened. You really
have caused us all a great deal of trouble and worry,
you know.'

Teena hung her head in shame. Miss Shimmery's
quiet words seared through her.

'Miss Shimmery, wait,' burst out Twink. 'I – I think
I'm to blame as well.' Teena looked up in surprise.

'Oh?' said Miss Shimmery, raising an eyebrow.

Twink nodded guiltily. 'You see, I was so wrapped
up in my Weather Magic project over the hols that I
ignored Teena. I was going to spend more time with

her this term, but – well, I put it off.' Twink's cheeks reddened. 'Anyway, I'm sure that she wouldn't have made such a silly wish if she hadn't been feeling cross with me.'

'But Twink, it wasn't *your* fault!' exclaimed Teena. 'I mean – well, it's true that I was a bit cross with you, but . . .' She shook her head, not sure what she wanted to say.

'Consequences again,' pointed out Miss Shimmery softly. 'But Twink, Teena is right – it's not your fault that she made her wish. She has to take responsibility for her own actions.'

Turning back to Teena, Miss Shimmery went on, 'As punishment, you will lose your free time for the next four weeks. You'll also write me an essay on the importance of always casting precise spells – and avoiding human magic!' Miss Shimmery paused as her words hung in the air. 'And Teena, I think it would be wise to keep your part in this episode quiet from the rest of the school.'

Teena let out a breath. 'Oh Miss Shimmery, *thank you*!' she burst out. 'I'll write you a brilliant essay, I promise! And Zuzu and Summer won't tell anyone, if I ask them not to.'

'Good,' said Miss Shimmery, patting Teena's shoulder. 'And now, I think we've all had enough drama for one day. Let's join the rest of the school, and go inside.'

Once the teachers had cast the complicated spell that protected Glitterwings and its surroundings, the students joyfully flew back to the school in long, colourful streams, chatting and laughing in the moonlight.

'Here, ah – I'll take Sal,' said Mr Woodleaf to Twink, picking up the salamander's lead. 'And well done for going after him, you two. I'm, ah – proud of you,' he mumbled.

Twink and Bimi exchanged a smile as Mr Woodleaf flew off towards the Creature Kindness log, with Sal trotting along below. *Good old Mr Woodleaf!* thought Twink. It made her feel warm inside to know that he was pleased with her.

She and Bimi started off. It was fully dark now,

with thousands of stars twinkling in the sky.

'Isn't it beautiful!' said Bimi, tipping her head back. She had been reunited with Chirpy, and held his cage gently under one arm. 'I'm so glad that things are really back to normal now.'

'Not as glad as I am!' said Teena, fluttering up alongside them. Moonlight glinted on her lavender wings. 'Twink, thanks for sticking up for me,' she added. 'But it really *wasn't* your fault, you know!'

'No, I suppose not,' said Twink ruefully. 'But I'm sorry anyway, Teena. I don't blame you for feeling fed up when you made your wish – I was a real moss brain over the hols!'

'Just don't dabble in wishes again, Teena, no matter *how* fed up you get,' put in Bimi with a smile. 'Unless you're trying to rival Sooze's record for getting into trouble!'

'Don't worry!' groaned Teena, linking her arm through Twink's. 'I've had enough excitement now to last me all year.'

The tree beckoned them forward, its windows gleaming with golden light. Suddenly Bimi giggled.

'You know what, Twink – we're going to have to do our Weather Magic project all over again. I don't think magical snowstorms really count!'

Twink slapped her forehead with a laugh. 'Oh no, you're right! Teena, would you like to help me with Sal?' she added eagerly.

Teena grinned and shook her head. 'I'd love to – but I've got an essay to write, remember?'

'Well, we'll do something else together soon,' said Twink, squeezing Teena's arm. 'That's a promise!'

The three fairies fluttered through the open front doors. Glitterwings towered above them, safe and warm. Students swooped in and out of its branches, delighted to be back where they belonged.

A second-year girl started to sing. Soon the whole school was taking up the song, their voices ringing through the winter night:

> *Oh, Glitterwings, dear Glitterwings,*
> *Beloved oak tree scho-ool.*
> *Good fairy fun for everyone,*
> *That is our fairy ru-ule.*
> *Our teachers wise,*
> *Their magic strong,*
> *With all our friends,*
> *We can't go wrong.*
> *Oh, Glitterwings, dear Glitterwings,*
> *Beloved oak tree scho-ool!*

Twink sighed happily as the song finished. With her best friend and sister, she flew towards the Great Branch. Their long-overdue dinner was awaiting them, along with all their friends.

Another term at Glitterwings had begun – and with any luck, thought Twink, it wouldn't be exciting at all!

To find out about other
glimmery Glitterwings
Academy stories,
turn over the page

Titania Woods

There are lots more stories about Glitterwings
Academy – make sure you haven't missed any of them!

If you have any difficulty in finding these in your local bookshop,
please visit www.bloomsbury.com or call 020 7440 2475
to order direct from Bloomsbury Publishing.

Visit www.glitterwingsacademy.co.uk for more fabulous fairy fun!